Night Goes By

By Kate Spohn

Macmillan Books for Young Readers • New York

Clouds are off playing
somewhere,
so Sun is on all day
with no nap.

Tired and ready for a rest,
Sun is happy to see Moon,
who is just glowing awake.

Sun is sinking with sleepiness.

"Good night,"
he calls out to Moon
before falling asleep.

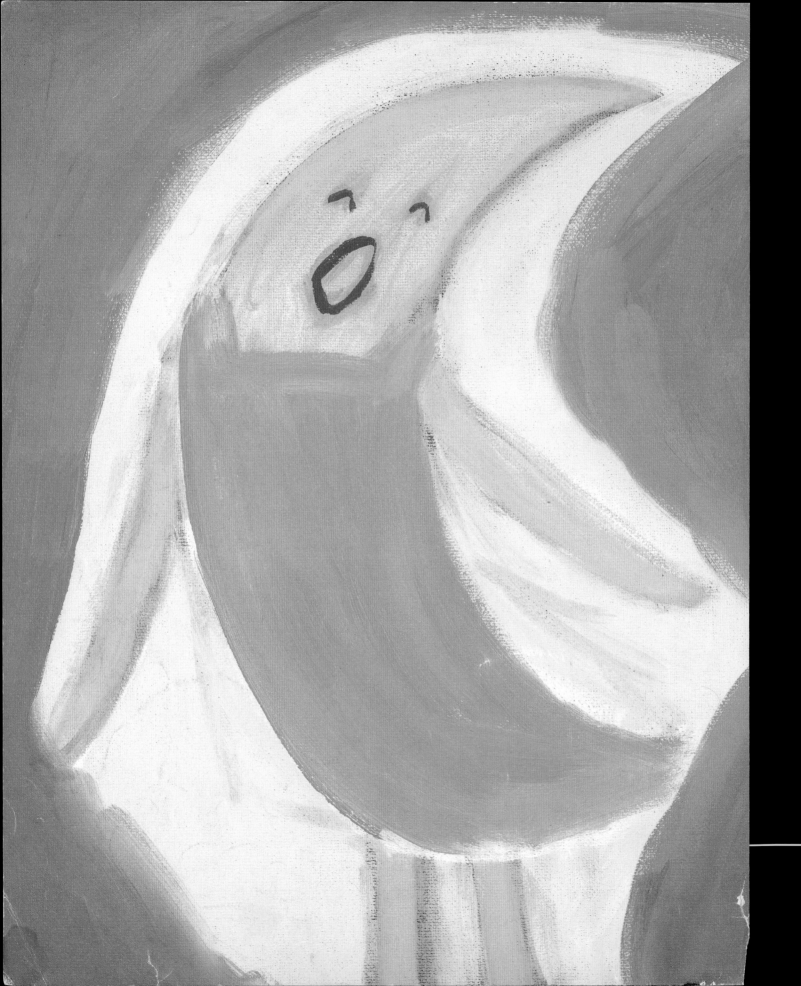

Moon is wide-awake and ready
to take over the sky.
"Star light, star bright,
I wish I may,
I wish I might,
I wish to have
this wish tonight!"
Moon sings
and wishes
her favorite star
would wake and join her.

Star wakes up.
She stretches until
she is feeling perky.

She visits her friend Moon.
Moon is happy to see Star.

Clouds pass by.
"Time for bed!"
they say, and wave good-bye.

Star does four cartwheels
and Moon laughs.
Star laughs, too.

Moon and Star dance
all night.

"How quickly
the night goes by,"
says Moon to Star.

Star is fading.
She says good night
to Moon.

Moon is sleepy, too.
She is happy
to see Sun.

"Good morning,"
Moon calls out to Sun
before falling asleep.

Sun is wide-awake
and ready
to take over the sky.

"Good morning!"
he tells everyone.

To my father,
who when I was a child
sang to me,
"You are my sunshine…"

Macmillan Books for Young Readers
An imprint of Simon & Schuster Children's Publishing Division

Simon & Schuster Macmillan
1230 Avenue of the Americas
New York, New York 10020

Designed by Julie Quan.
The text of this book is set in Clearface.
The illustrations were done in oil.
Printed and bound in Singapore on recycled paper.

First edition
10 9 8 7 6 5 4 3 2 1

LIBRARY OF CONGRESS CATALOGING-IN-PUBLICATION DATA
Spohn, Kate.
Night goes by / Written and illustrated by Kate Spohn.
p.   cm.
Summary: Sun, Moon, and Star visit one another and take turns
shining in the sky.
ISBN 0-02-786351-4
[1. Sun—Fiction.   2. Moon—Fiction.   3. Stars—Fiction.]
I. Title.
PZ7.S7636Ni   1995
[E]—dc20   94-19312